www.FlowerpotPress.com
DJS-0912-0178
ISBN: 978-1-4867-1467-4
Made in China/Fabriqué en Chine

Positively
Purple

Written by Linda Ragsdale
Illustrated by P.S. Brooks

PB and Jeli were best bear
friends who loved to play together.

Visitors at the zoo would whistle and whoop as PB and Jeli played ball.

Until one day when PB threw
the ball and it didn't come back.

So, PB waited...

And the visitors waited...

But there was no ball and no Jeli.

Jeli was sick.

The zookeeper came
and she called the nutritionist.
The nutritionist came
and she called the zoo director.
The zoo director came
and he called the doctor.
The doctor came
and he gave Jeli some medicine.
Jeli felt better.

Better and...

"PURPLE!" Jeli shrieked.
"Look at me! NO, don't look at me! The medicine turned me purple! I feel better... But I can't be seen like this! I can't let the visitors see me like this!"

Jeli tried to RUB off the purple.

She tried to SCRUB off the purple.

She even tried to PAINT on some white.

But Jeli stayed ABSOLUTELY purple.

Jeli's friends came to visit her.
Pinky strutted in with fabulous flamingo flair.

"Who CARES what color you are?
You just be YOU!" she said.
"I'm proudly pink. Show the world the purple you!"

Petey pushed past Pinky
and splayed a splendid tail
of shimmery blues, greens,
and purples.

"Look at ME! When I stand this
way, I'm blue. When I turn this way,
I'm green. Why are you hiding in this
cave? Look at YOU! You're exquisite!
You need to parade this new hue of
purple you!"

Carlos strolled in to see Jeli.

He changed color five times as he crossed the room.

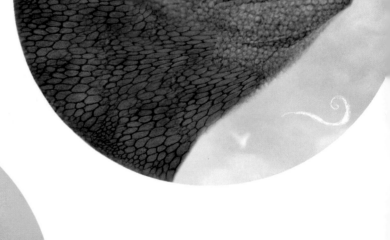

Green to blue to red to orange and even purple.

"CHANGE IS GOOD!"
he said. "You'll see."

Jeli thought of her friends.
She didn't feel fabulously pink.
She didn't feel shimmery blue.

And she couldn't keep changing colors.
She could, however, change one thing...
She could change her attitude.

So she did just that!

"I'm going to be THE MOST AMAZING purple bear!" Jeli declared. "I'm going to be ABSOLUTELY, POSITIVELY PURPLE!"

From that moment on, Jeli was back to being Jeli.

Jeli RAN purple.

Jeli SWAM purple.

Jeli LAUGHED and PLAYED and even did a HANDSTAND purple.

And the visitors changed
something too...

Some days you'll feel PROUDLY pink.
Some days you'll be BOLDLY blue.
Some days you WON'T know how you feel.

But with a good attitude and some good friends, you can turn any day into an ABSOLUTELY, POSITIVELY PURPLE day!

This book is lovingly dedicated to all those facing any challenge at any age. I hope it inspires a positively purple attitude to help give you strength on your journey. It is specially dedicated to my friend Jessica Meyer, who at just eleven years old demonstrated to me an amazingly positively purple attitude. I'm thrilled to be honoring her spirit in this story too!